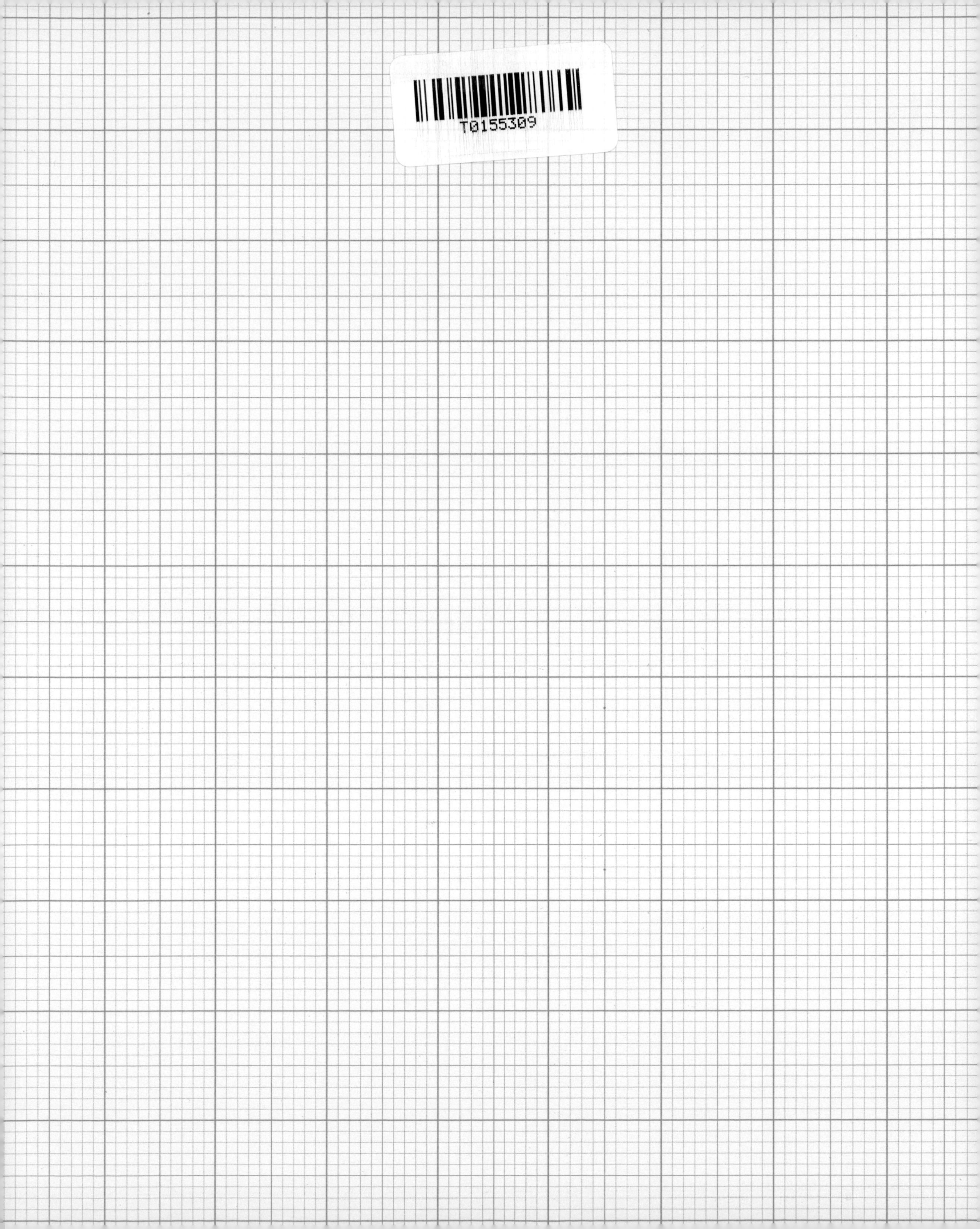
T0155309

IGGY
PECK,
ARCHITECT

Illustrator's Note: The illustrations in this book were made with watercolors, pen, and ink on Arches paper. For some pieces, pencil and graph paper were also employed.

Library of Congress Cataloging-in-Publication Data:

Beaty, Andrea.
Iggy Peck, architect / by Andrea Beaty ;
illustrated by David Roberts.
p. cm.
Summary: Ever since he was a baby, Iggy Peck has built towers, bridges, and buildings, which comes in handy when his second grade class is stranded on an island during a picnic.
ISBN 978-0-8109-1106-2

[1. Building—Fiction.
2. Schools—Fiction.
3. School field trips—Fiction.
4. Stories in rhyme.]
I. Roberts, David, 1970- ill. II. Title.

PZ8.3.B38447Ig 2007
[E]—dc22
2006013574

Text copyright © 2007 Andrea Beaty
Illustrations copyright © 2007 David Roberts

Book design by Chad W. Beckerman

Published in 2007 by Abrams Books for Young Readers, an imprint of ABRAMS. All rights reserved. No portion of this book may be reproduced, stored in a retrieval system, or transmitted in any form or by any means, mechanical, electronic, photocopying, recording, or otherwise, without written permission from the publisher.

Printed and bound in China
46 45

Abrams Books for Young Readers are available at special discounts when purchased in quantity for premiums and promotions as well as fundraising or educational use. Special editions can also be created to specification. For details, contact specialsales@abramsbooks.com or the address below.

ABRAMS The Art of Books
195 Broadway, New York, NY 10007
abramsbooks.com

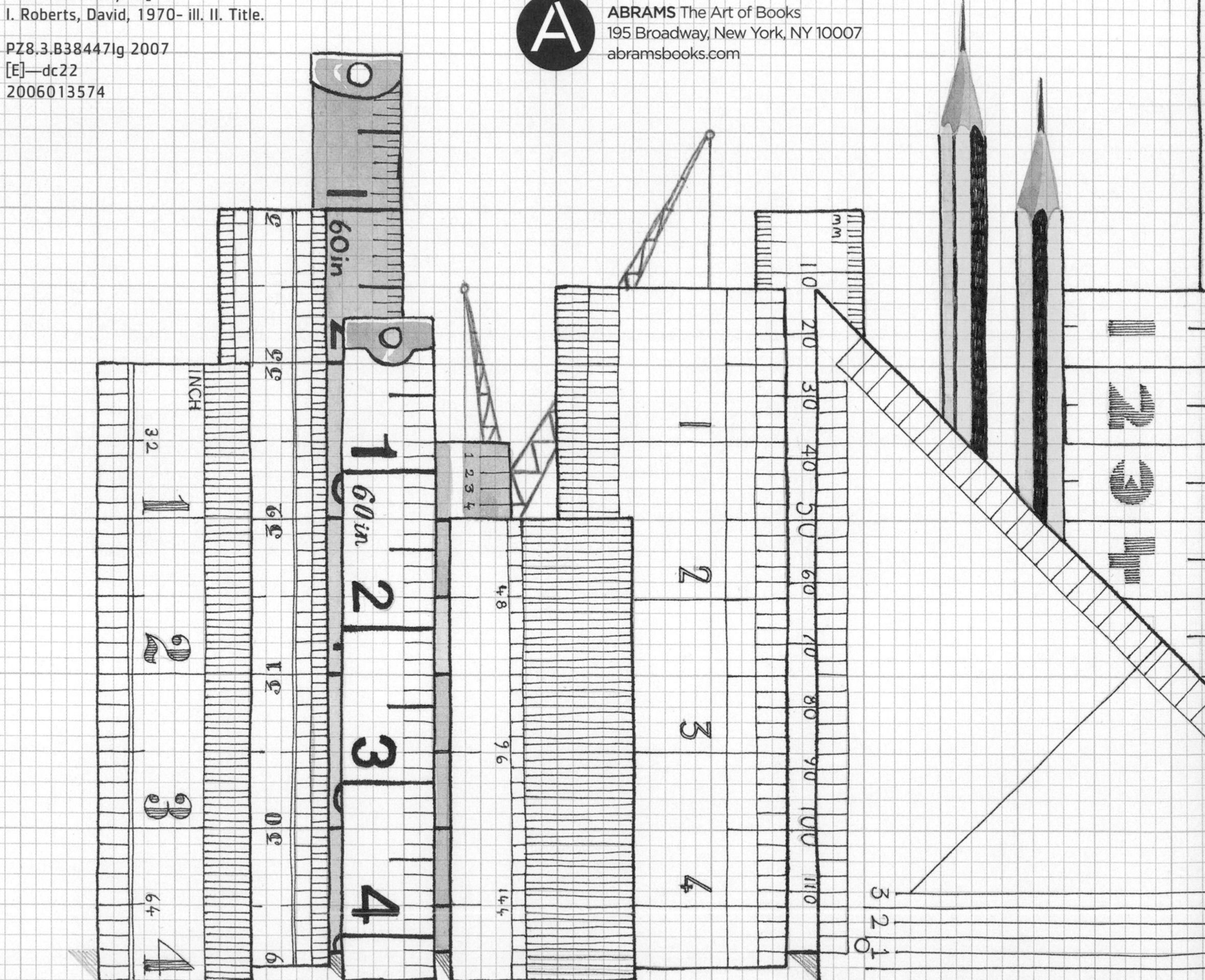

TO ANDREW, WHO INSPIRES ME–A.B.

FOR CHRISTOPHER–D.R.

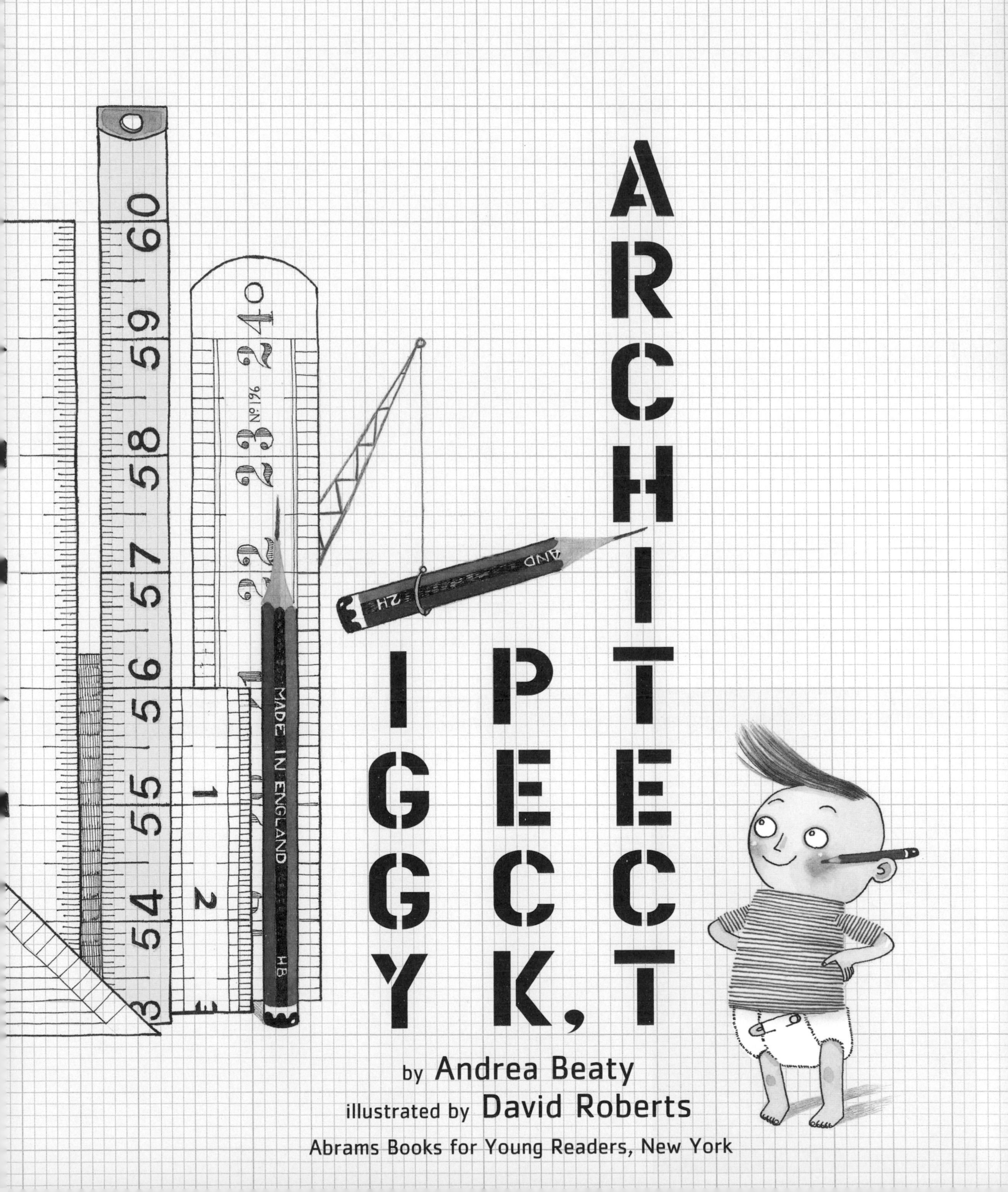

IGGY PECK, ARCHITECT

by Andrea Beaty

illustrated by David Roberts

Abrams Books for Young Readers, New York

YOUNG IGGY PECK IS AN ARCHITECT
and has been since he was two,
when he built a great tower—in only an hour—
with nothing but diapers and glue.

"Good Gracious, Ignacious!" his mother exclaimed.

"That's the coolest thing I've ever seen!"

But her smile faded fast as a light wind blew past

and she realized those diapers weren't clean!

"Ignacious, my son! What on Earth have you done?

That's disgusting and nasty! It stinks!"

But Iggy was gone. He was out on the lawn
using dirt clods to build a great Sphinx.

When Iggy was three, his parents could see
his unusual passion would stay.
He built churches and chapels from peaches and apples,
and temples from modeling clay.

At dinner one night, to his father's delight,
Iggy got a bright gleam in his eye
and out on the porch built the St. Louis Arch
from pancakes and coconut pie.

ARC
HIT
ECTU
RE
ROMANESQUE
GOTHIC
GOTHIC
Modern
EMPIRE

Dear Ig had it made until second grade,
when his teacher was Miss Lila Greer.
On the very first day, she had this to say:
"We do not talk of buildings in here!

Gothic or Romanesque, I couldn't care less
about buildings—ancient or new."
She said in her lecture about architecture
that it had no place in grade two.

That might seem severe, but she was sincere.
For when she was no more than seven,
she'd had a great fright at a dizzying height
in a building so tall it scraped Heaven.

On an architect's tour of the ninety-fifth floor,
young Lila got lost from the group.

58 59 60 61 62
53 54 55 56 57
48 49 50 51 52
43 44 45 46 47
38 39 40 41 42
33 34 35 36 37
26 27 28 29 30 31 32
17 18 19 20 21 22 23 24 25
8 9 10 11 12 13 14 15 16
B G 1 2 3 4 5 6 7

She was found two days later in a stuck elevator,
eating cheese with a French circus troupe.

After that day—it's quite safe to say—
she thought all building-lovers were nuts.
As a teacher she taught that, above all, one ought
to avoid them. No *if*s, *and*s, or *but*s!

As you might guess, it would cause Iggy stress
to hear such terrible talk.
But he didn't hear. He sat in the rear
while building a castle of chalk.

"You! Iggy Peck! Your desk is a wreck!
Tear down that castle right now!
You will not build in here. Is that perfectly clear?
Do you need to see Principal Howe?"

"No, Ma'am," Iggy said. He lowered his head,

and his heart sank down to the floor.

With no chance to build, his interest was killed.

Now second grade was a bore.

After twelve long days that passed in a haze of reading, writing, and arithmetic,

Miss Greer took the class to Blue River Pass for a hike and an old-fashioned picnic.

They crossed an old trestle to a small island nestled
in the heart of a burbling stream.
But they no sooner passed than the
footbridge collapsed
and Miss Lila Greer
started to
scream,
"We're trapped here! Oh my! Alas, kids, good-bye!"
Her eyeballs rolled back in her head.
She dropped to the ground with a vague groaning sound.
(Luckily fainted—not dead.)

The class was amazed. They stood there quite dazed,
uncertain of what they should do.
But one bright young man was off hatching a plan,
which started with Miss Lila's shoe.

Soon each lad and lass there at Blue River Pass
was working together as one.

And when she came to, Miss Lila Greer knew
that something quite brave had been done.

She looked in the air and saw hanging there
a structure with cables and braces.
And on the far side—beaming with pride—
were seventeen smiling young faces.

Boots, tree roots and strings, fruit roll-ups and things
(some of which one should not mention)
were stretched ridge to ridge in a glorious bridge
dangling from shoestring suspension.

It all became clear to Miss Lila Greer,
as she crossed that bridge over the stream.
There are worse things to do when you're in grade two
than to spend your time building a dream.

746 feet high
4200 feet

Now every week at Blue River Creek
Elementary in second grade,
all the schoolkids can hear, along with Miss Greer,
how the world's greatest buildings were made.

The weekly guest speaker, in T-shirt and sneakers,
talks of buildings from Rome to Quebec.
Of course, he's the guy who builds towers from pie,
that brilliant young man, Iggy Peck.

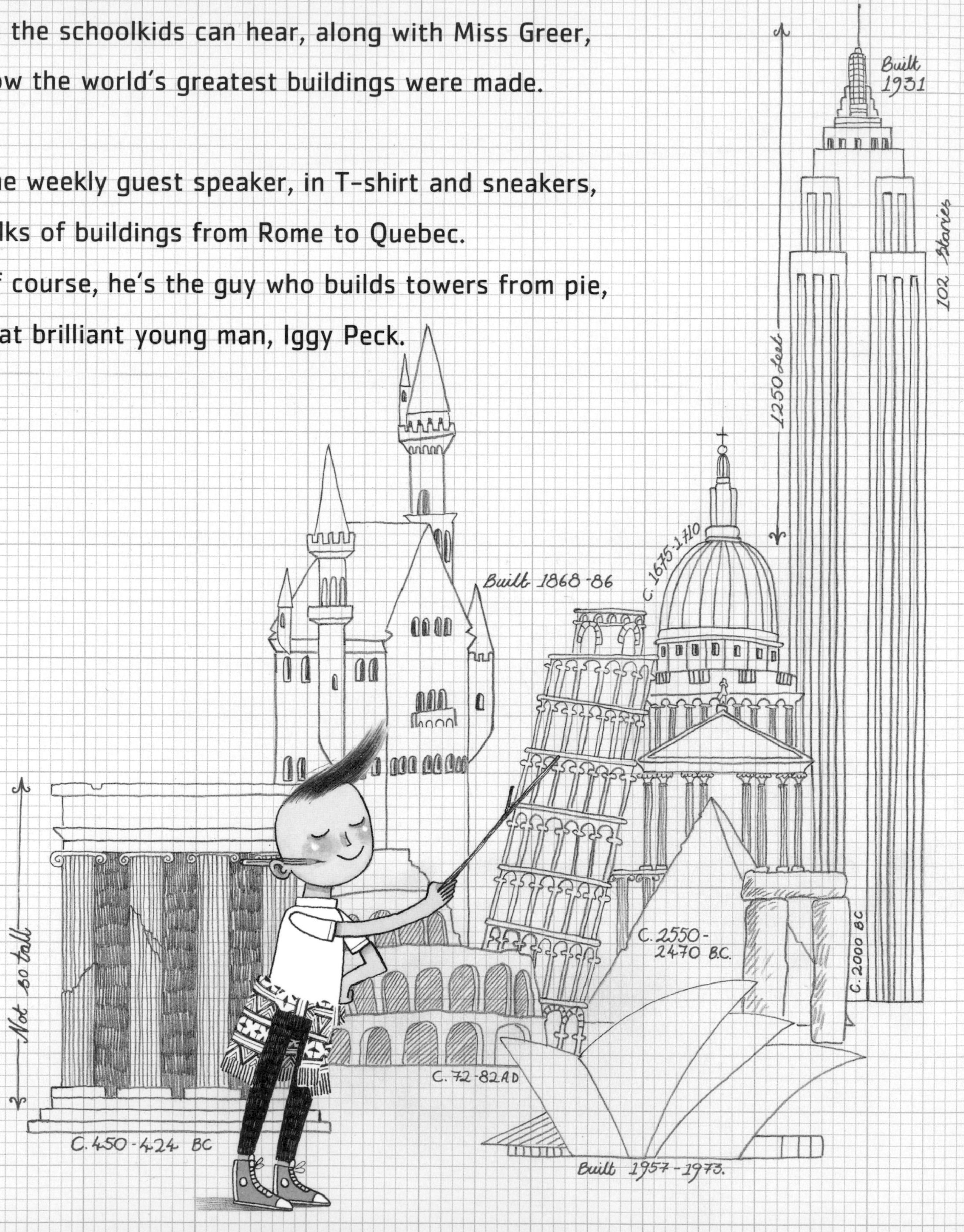